AF270510

ESSENTIAL **FITNESS**

AEROBIC EXERCISE

BY KAITLIN SCIRRI

Essential Library

An Imprint of Abdo Publishing
abdobooks.com

ABDOBOOKS.COM

Published by Abdo Publishing, a division of ABDO, PO Box 398166, Minneapolis, Minnesota 55439. Copyright © 2025 by Abdo Consulting Group, Inc. International copyrights reserved in all countries. No part of this book may be reproduced in any form without written permission from the publisher. Essential Library™ is a trademark and logo of Abdo Publishing.

Printed in the United States of America, North Mankato, Minnesota.
052024
092024

Cover Photo: Ljupco Smokovski/Shutterstock Images
Interior Photos: People Images/iStockphoto, 3, 35, 36, 48, 78; Srdjan Pav/iStockphoto, 4–5; Wavebreak Media Ltd/Alamy, 7; Shutterstock Images, 9, 12–13, 20–21, 32, 40, 44, 46, 62, 74, 77, 81, 88–89, 92, 94, 101; iStockphoto, 10, 42, 55, 56–57, 65, 69, 72, 90, 99; Hulton Archive/Getty Images, 14; Gregory Lee/Fairfax Media Archives/Getty Images, 18; Finnbarr Webster Editorial/Alamy, 21; John Phillips/EMPPL PA Wire/AP Images, 23; Ted Shaffrey/AP Images, 24; Slawomir Kruz/Shutterstock Images, 26; Jacob Lund/Shutterstock Images, 29, 38; Odua Images/Shutterstock Images, 31; Alliance Images/Shutterstock Images, 41; Tetra Images/Alamy, 51; Ruslan Dashinsky/iStockphoto, 59, 100; Egoitz Bengoetxea/Shutterstock Images, 66–67; Val Thoermer/Alamy, 70; Pierre Jean Durieu/Shutterstock Images, 83; Teran Studios/Shutterstock Images, 86; Boris Riaposov/Shutterstock Images, 96

Editor: Charlie Beattie
Series Designer: Jake Slavik

Library of Congress Control Number: 2023949398

PUBLISHER'S CATALOGING-IN-PUBLICATION DATA
Names: Scirri, Kaitlin, author.
Title: Aerobic exercise / by Kaitlin Scirri
Description: Minneapolis, Minnesota: Abdo Publishing, 2025 | Series: Essential fitness | Includes online resources and index.
Identifiers: ISBN 9781098293277 (lib. bdg.) | ISBN 9798384912545 (ebook)
Subjects: LCSH: Aerobic exercises--Juvenile literature. | Workouts (Exercise)--Juvenile literature. | Physical activity--Juvenile literature. | Muscles--Juvenile literature. | Exercise--Juvenile literature. | Physical fitness--Juvenile literature.
Classification: DDC 613.71--dc23

CONTENTS

WORK IT OUT

Hannah was not a morning person. When the alarm sounded on her phone at 6:00 a.m., she wanted to hit the snooze option. Instead, she swiped the alarm off and threw back the covers. Then she heard the familiar "ping" sound of a text message. Hannah knew who it was. Her best friend, Alyson, was also rising early so they could do a virtual workout together. Hannah typed out a quick text back to Alyson: "I'm up!"

Doing aerobics in the morning was a new idea for Hannah. She was too embarrassed to take an in-person aerobics class. She had never been very athletic or coordinated. What if kids from school showed up? What if she couldn't keep up with the rest of the class? Would they make fun of her for being out of shape?

An estimated 46.9 percent of US adults get the recommended weekly amount of aerobic exercise.

Hannah was usually in the library rather than on the sports field. She was a high achiever and had earned a spot in the National Honor Society because of her grades. She also participated in several clubs, including the school newspaper and yearbook club. While Hannah enjoyed her activities, she often felt stressed. Sometimes homework, studying, and the pressure of looking ahead to college felt overwhelming. Her guidance counselor thought exercise would be a good way to manage the stress. The counselor suggested making it fun, such as taking a dance aerobics class. Hannah was nervous about trying a class with other people. And gym memberships were expensive. So she was trying an app at home.

A virtual aerobics class was the perfect solution for Hannah. She didn't have to worry about anyone else watching. She wouldn't feel self-conscious. Through the aerobics app and FaceTime, she was able to work out with a friend in the comfort of her own home.

Hannah got out of bed and changed into yoga pants, a sports bra, and a fitted T-shirt. Aerobics requires big movements, and these comfortable clothes allowed her to move around without restrictions. She tied her sneakers and pulled her hair into a ponytail. Her house was quiet this early in the morning. After stopping in the kitchen for water and a granola bar, Hannah headed into the living room. She pushed the coffee table off to the side so she had more space to move around.

Before the class began, Hannah needed to warm up. Slowly elevating her heart rate would signal to her body that it was time for a workout. She rose up and down on the balls of her feet to flex her calves. She twisted her

torso from left to right and swung her arms around in big circles. She drank more water. It was important to hydrate before, during, and after her workouts. But drinking water too fast could result in swallowing air and making her bloated and uncomfortable, so she took small sips.

Hannah powered on her TV and gaming console then selected her "Get Fit with Dance Hits" app. Propping her phone up by the TV, she FaceTimed Alyson.

"Hey, girl!" Alyson answered. "You ready?"

"I think so," Hannah yawned.

"Come on! You've got this. *We've* got this!" A benefit to having a virtual workout partner in Alyson was that they encouraged one another and held each other accountable.

Hannah smiled as she scrolled through the workout options. "I'm thinking something energetic this morning. I'm pretty anxious about my math test later this week. I need to work off the stress."

"Sounds perfect. How about *Morning Motivation?*"

Listening to music while exercising has been proven to extend the amount of time spent working out.

"Let's do it!" Both girls selected the same workout in the app and took their positions in front of their TVs as the music began playing.

The instructor led the girls through the workout, which started slowly before growing more intense. As the beat sped up, so did their heart rates. Hannah felt her limbs loosen up as she moved to the music, lifting her arms and her legs. She began taking deep breaths in and out, breathing faster with the increased effort. The harder she worked, the more oxygen her muscles needed. She could feel her pulse accelerate as her heart worked to pump blood throughout her body.

Aerobics can be an effective way to relieve tension and stress, according to the Anxiety & Depression Association of America.

"Whew! This one's a burner!" Alyson yelled breathlessly from her side of the video call. "I'm panting and sweating already!"

"Remember what . . . the instructor . . . says . . ." Hannah answered, finding it difficult to talk as she moved to the music. "It's always . . . tough . . . at first." Hannah and Alyson knew they had to build up their stamina. They had to work out slowly at first, gradually increasing the length and intensity of their routines.

REAPING THE REWARDS

After 30 minutes of dancing, the instructor announced the end of the workout. It was time to cool down.

Hannah welcomed a few sips of water and dabbed beads of sweat from her forehead. She felt her heart rate gradually slow as she moved back and forth across the living room, breathing deeply and stretching.

She felt much more awake than she had when the alarm sounded. Aerobics releases a rush of endorphins, and Hannah was already feeling their effects. She felt energized and excited for the day. She also felt proud of herself for choosing to get up and work out instead of sleeping a little longer.

After just two weeks of regular workouts, Hannah could tell the difference. She was less stressed. Working out gave her an outlet, a chance to relieve stress instead of letting it build up inside. The movements and exertion gave her a physical way to release her emotions and worries before they affected her in a negative way. Instead of stressing out, she had learned to work it out through aerobics.

GRAB YOUR GEAR

Aerobics can be done with little or no equipment. However, equipment can be a great way to add some variety to an everyday aerobics routine. Popular aerobics equipment includes hand weights, jump ropes, and Hula-Hoops. Step aerobics requires a step platform. Water aerobics may include water weights, a kickboard, a pool noodle, goggles, and water shoes. Rowing can be done with a rowing machine or resistance bands.

WHAT IS AEROBIC EXERCISE?

Every day, people all over the world exercise. Many of them choose to do things such as running, biking, or participating in a dance class. These activities are all forms of aerobic exercise. When people are doing aerobics, they are performing exercises that cause an increase in oxygen intake. The word *aerobic* means "with oxygen." This type of exercise involves using oxygen to power the muscles.

Swimming, walking, and biking are forms of low-impact aerobics. They are less strenuous on the joints than high-impact aerobics, such as running. Dancing can be low impact or high impact, depending on the movements.

Though commonly associated with movement-based fitness classes, aerobic exercise can take many forms

American runner John Hayes, *right*, approaches the finish line at the 1908 Olympic Games in London, England.

AEROBIC VS. ANAEROBIC

Aerobics is often linked with cardiovascular exercise, or cardio for short. Cardiovascular exercise refers to exercise that raises the heart rate. Aerobics and cardio often overlap because they both trigger an increase in cardiovascular activity. But aerobic exercise causes an increase in both heart rate and breathing, which helps to increase oxygen intake to power the muscles.

However, there are cardio exercises that increase heart rate without increasing oxygen intake to power the workout. These exercises are called anaerobic exercises. *Anaerobic* means "without oxygen," and it includes exercises such as weight lifting, sprinting, and high-intensity interval training. During an anaerobic workout, the heart rate increases. However, the body relies on stored energy to power the workout instead of an increase in oxygen.

A HISTORY OF AEROBICS

Aerobic exercises have been used for recreation as well as for sport for centuries. Certain aerobic activities, such as walking and running, have always existed. For most of human history, they were primarily used for transportation rather than fitness or competition. With the invention of the bicycle and automobile, people have relied less on foot transportation and have turned to machines.

Bicycling is another aerobic activity that was initially used as a means of transportation before becoming a sports or fitness activity. Today bicycling is used for transportation, leisure, and fitness.

The first modern Olympic Games were held in Athens, Greece, in 1896. They featured competitions in swimming and cycling. Today's Olympic Games feature aerobic sports such as swimming, rowing, cycling, running, racewalking, and figure skating.

AEROBICS FOR FITNESS

Aerobic exercise has been a popular form of physical fitness for decades. The idea to use aerobics as a means to improve physical health and prevent disease was introduced by a doctor named Kenneth H. Cooper. The term was first used by Cooper in his 1968 book *Aerobics*.

In 1977, he published a second book titled *The Aerobics Way*. In his books, Cooper examined different exercises for different age groups. His medical research explained the role aerobics played in helping people live longer, healthier lives by preventing disease. Cooper also stressed the importance of working out regularly. Cooper said, "We do not stop exercising because we grow old—we grow old because we stop exercising."[2]

Both books became popular, which helped create an aerobics movement in the United States. People became aware of the positive impact aerobic exercise had on their health, such as improving their heart health and increasing their life spans. As a result of Cooper's research, aerobics classes became common. They were usually offered in health clubs and gyms, where an aerobics instructor would lead a group of people through exercises to upbeat music.

Because of their popularity, different kinds of aerobic exercises began to appear. Aerobic Dance was created in 1969 by Jacki Sorensen. That same year, Judi Sheppard Missett created Jazzercise, a fitness activity that combines aerobics with jazz dance movements. Both forms of aerobics became popular because they created a lively alternative to walking, running, or biking.

When videocassette recorders became common in the 1980s, they created a new wave of the

Dr. Kenneth H. Cooper, *right*, instructs a man on how to use a rowing machine at the University of New South Wales in Australia in 1974.

aerobics movement. People could purchase videotapes of workout programs to exercise at home. The ability to work out at home instead of going to a fitness center dramatically altered aerobics. People no longer had to pay a membership fee or find the time to go to the gym to get fit. "Redefining exercise beyond calisthenics, weight lifting, and organized sport—and as an activity appropriate for everyone—was revolutionary," says historian Natalia Mehlman Petrzela.[3]

Fitness expert Gin Miller introduced Step Aerobics in the late 1980s. Over the next decade, it steadily grew in popularity. Also known as Step Training or simply Step, it was a form of aerobics that used the movement of stepping up and down to get fit. Each participant had an individual step in front of them, roughly two feet (61 cm) long. The height of each step was between ten and 12 inches (25–30 cm).

The fitness program was popular because it was low impact. It was a less challenging workout for those who were recovering from injuries or new to physical fitness. Step Aerobics is still popular today, and the latest versions of steps are often adjustable, usually anywhere from four to 12 inches (10–30 cm) in height.

FITNESS TRACKERS

In 1965, Japanese doctor Yoshiro Hatano created what he called the Manpo-kei, which translates to "10,000 steps meter." It started a revolution in how people can track their fitness goals. Today, these types of devices are known as fitness trackers, and they come in many forms. They can be wearable devices, such as a smartwatch, or apps that are downloaded to a phone or tablet.

Wearable devices are popular with exercisers because many can automatically track and record a workout. Many fitness trackers have Global Positioning System (GPS) capability, allowing someone to map their workout. If someone goes for a walk, a run, or a ride, the GPS tracker can show them where they are and map where they've been.

A tracker measures blood flow near a wearer's wrist to monitor heart rate. It collects data on a person's basal metabolic rate (BMR). The tracker can then collect workout data when that person is active. Once it has both sets of information, it can compare the wearer's workout data to the BMR in order to estimate how many calories a person is burning while working out.

Fitbit has sold more than
100 million wearable devices
since the company launched
its first fitness band in 2009.

Fitness trackers are not just convenient ways to track workouts but have contributed to increased physical activity among people who use them. On average, people who wear fitness trackers take approximately 1,200 more steps per day than those who do not. The most popular fitness trackers are wearable devices, with Apple products leading the industry. Since 2017, Apple has dominated the wearable fitness tracker market, with around 146 million wearable devices shipped in 2022.[4]

Step was not the only aerobics craze to gain prominence in the 1990s. Tae Bo is a combination of karate moves, boxing, and aerobic dance moves. Developed by former competitive martial artist Billy Blanks, the fitness program became wildly popular in the 1990s. Previous aerobics programs, such as Aerobic Dance and Jazzercise, largely appealed to women, but Tae Bo became popular with men as well. The workouts were high energy and offered feelings of strength and empowerment due to their karate and boxing moves.

Fitness instructor and choreographer Alberto "Beto" Pérez created the dance workout program Zumba in the 1990s. By the early 2000s, Zumba had become well-known, and classes were highly sought after. Zumba classes offered an aerobic workout that included dance moves from Caribbean, South American, and Indian cultures. By 2012, there were 100,000 Zumba instructors teaching the popular courses in more than 125 countries.[5] "Ultimately, we saw that the person that was most passionate about our brand was our instructors and we made them our partner[s] and that is what allowed us to grow," says Zumba Fitness cofounder Alberto Perlman.[6]

When smartphones began dominating the cell phone market around 2010, another aerobics craze took off. Fitness apps for smartphones tracked step counts, allowing people to see how many steps they took per day.

Zumba founder Beto Pérez, *center*, leads a class in London, England, in 2016.

This daily counter motivated many to begin or increase their aerobic exercise through walking. Walking continues to be one of the most popular forms of aerobic exercise.

INSPIRING AN INDUSTRY

As aerobics increased in popularity, the demand for aerobics equipment and accessories also grew. Production of items such as footwear, swimwear, and exercise machines skyrocketed. Some companies focused on workout clothing. Instead of cotton T-shirts, fitness buffs could work out in clothing that absorbs sweat and prevents people from overheating while working out.

The Nike "Moon Shoe" was created by Oregon track coach Bill Bowerman in 1972. He made its innovative gripping sole by molding the rubber on his kitchen waffle iron.

Running shoes were one of the first aerobics-related industries to take off. The first patent for lightweight rubber-soled running shoes was issued in 1832 to New Yorker Wait Webster. But it would take another 130 years for the industry to boom.

In the early 1960s, runner Phil Knight and his former coach, Bill Bowerman, designed their own running shoes after realizing that nothing on the market met their needs. They created their own company, which eventually became known as Nike. Nike became the leading seller of running shoes throughout the 1970s. The company remains the number one seller of athletic footwear, making billions of dollars each year.[7]

AEROBICS GEAR

The right apparel and equipment are important for any type of aerobic exercise. That often means finding the right clothing, shoes, and protective gear. Bicyclists often look for padded shorts to provide comfort when sitting for long stretches in the bike's saddle. Bike frames also come in different and often adjustable sizes. Many bikes, both outdoor road cycles and indoor stationary models, require special shoes that clip into the pedals. If biking outdoors, a helmet is a recommended safety precaution. However, in many US states a helmet is required when biking outdoors. Some outdoor bikers also wear gloves, elbow pads, and kneepads.

Swimming does not require much in the way of equipment, but there are few items that every swimmer should have. A comfortable bathing suit is key and should fit just right—not too loose but not so tight as to restrict movements or cause discomfort. A swim cap is required at many public pools, and goggles are a preferred accessory for many swimmers. Other items swimmers might use include a kickboard, aquatic weights, and a pool noodle or other flotation device. Water shoes may also be worn in pools, lakes, or the ocean.

Thirty-seven US states have some
form of bicycle helmet law in place.

Any aerobics done on land requires proper footwear for a comfortable workout, and the type of footwear will vary depending on the type of exercise. There are shoes or cleats designed specifically for walking, running, biking, and other forms of fitness. For all land exercises, the ideal shoes will have good support to cushion the wearer's feet. They should fit snugly enough that they don't slip or rub against the heel but provide enough flexibility to move freely.

Once the right shoes are fitted, they should be paired with proper socks. Socks worn during aerobics should be breathable, meaning they allow air to easily pass through the material. They should also wick moisture, which means they absorb sweat and dry quickly. The right combination of socks and shoes can prevent discomfort and injuries such as blisters.

As with socks, other clothing worn during aerobic exercise should be breathable and rapidly absorb moisture. A lightweight, breathable shirt will help keep a person cool while working out. Pants should allow comfortable movement. They should be fitted but not so tight as to restrict movement or cause friction against skin, as this can cause discomfort and even leave marks or rashes.

Appropriate shoes are critical for a successful run, and the location where someone is planning to run makes a difference in the type of shoe they should wear. Road running shoes are great for paved streets, sidewalks, tracks, or treadmills. Trail running shoes are designed for those who like to run off-road on trails. They have stronger grip to prevent slipping on dirt paths or in mud. Cross-training shoes are for those who prefer the gym and like to mix up their workouts, as cross-trainers can be worn for running or other exercise routines.

Whichever environment is chosen, the shoe should fit comfortably without moving around or rubbing against the heel. People with high arches should be sure to get arch support in their shoes. This can be a specially designed shoe or an insert that goes inside the shoe. A lack of proper arch support can result in the feet flattening or inflammation of muscles and tendons in and around the foot.

Many people choose to run with a partner or in a group.

A SOCIAL EVENT

For many people, aerobics is a social activity. Aerobics classes are a fun way to be active, and they provide an opportunity to socialize with others. People can take classes with friends or make new friends all over the world during class. They have the opportunity to share their fitness journeys with one another. They can also use the community space to share encouragement and exchange success stories.

Aerobics can still be a social activity, even when people work out at home rather than with a group or a class. Virtual workout options give exercisers the chance to work out at the same time and check in with each other through cell phones or workout apps. Wearable fitness devices allow people to challenge each other and hold each other accountable.

AEROBICS TODAY

Many people practice aerobics today at gyms and fitness centers. There are many popular pieces of aerobics equipment. They include treadmills, ellipticals, stationary bikes, and step climbers.

Virtual aerobics workouts offer benefits that in-person workouts don't, making them the choice for many. Virtual workouts can be done at any time, which makes them convenient. Someone can open an app or website and work out whenever it fits into their schedule without having to work around gym hours or class times.

They also offer flexibility. If people travel often for work, they can take their apps and devices with them and keep up with their workouts while away from home. "Virtual fitness is here to stay because you can't beat the convenience," says trainer Emily Diers. "It allows you to put a trainer in your pocket while you travel. It serves up inspiration in a moment's notice when you need it."[9]

Elliptical machines are one of the many popular aerobic alternatives to walking or running.

AEROBICS AND THE BODY

Aerobics' effects on the body include improved physical strength, increased muscle, stronger bones, improved flexibility, and lower blood pressure. It can also improve sleep and reduce stress levels. Aerobics has effects on various muscle groups, as well as on organs such as the brain.

AEROBICS AND THE HEART

An aerobic workout provides exercise for the whole body, especially the heart. During an aerobic workout, the heart is strengthened, which allows for better blood flow throughout the body. Aerobic workouts also affect heart rate, both

Aerobic exercise offers a full-body workout.

immediately and in the long term. According to physician Kerry Stewart, "One of the key benefits of exercise is that it helps to control or modify many of the risk factors for heart disease."[1]

Active heart rate can occur during a workout, while resting heart rate is the number of times the heart beats per minute while someone is at rest. That does not necessarily mean lying down or sleeping. A resting heart rate simply means that the body is not currently active. Aerobic workouts are an effective way to speed up heart rate.

The immediate effect on the heart during aerobics is an increase in the number of beats per minute. As the workout progresses, the body needs more oxygen. A higher heart rate delivers this oxygen to cells and muscles that need it. But consistent workouts will eventually cause a person's resting heart rate to decrease. A lower resting heart rate is considered a sign that the heart is healthy and working well. The recommended resting heart rate varies

by age group. A healthy resting heart rate for adolescents ages 13 to 18 is 60 to 100 beats per minute.[2]

The heart is a muscle, and like other muscles in the body, it becomes stronger with regular exercise. However, it is important that people not compare their heart rate with each other. For example, someone's active heart rate during aerobic exercise may be different from that of their friend or teammate. That just means that their bodies are different. Working out is not a contest, and heart rates vary based on physical health and genetics.

BONES AND MUSCLES

Bones are more than just the framework of a body. They are made of living tissue consisting of protein, collagen, and minerals. Research has shown that a lack of physical activity can, over time, lead to a disease that causes bones to thin and shrink. This bone loss is called osteoporosis.

Higher-impact activities are believed to be more effective at slowing bone loss than lower-impact exercises.

Aerobic exercise can help prevent this by contributing to bone homeostasis, the body's natural process of maintaining bone health and strength. This can help prevent serious injury, such as broken bones. It's a great idea to start doing aerobics at a young age so the bones have more time to benefit from the workouts.

Muscles are tight bundles of stretchy fibers made of proteins. They are controlled by branches of specialized nerve cells. During exercise, muscles can become sore. The workout puts stress on muscle cells, which leads to what are called microtears. "Once these occur, the body sends good nutrition and good blood to the area to heal. This, in turn, is how you grow musculature," says surgeon Michael Karns.[3] The more aerobics a person does, the stronger their muscles become over time and with proper recovery. This helps prevent major muscle tears, which are serious injuries that need time to heal.

SLEEP BENEFITS AND STRESS RELIEF

Getting the right amount of sleep is critical to overall health. Sleep helps regulate blood pressure, the immune system, breathing, heart health, appetite, and mental health. Aerobic exercise has been shown to help people sleep better.

One of the simplest ways aerobics helps with sleep is that it is physically tiring. No matter the workout someone

Working out at night can be beneficial, but it is important to cool down before attempting to sleep.

chooses, they will be fatigued from the effort they put into it. Another way aerobics positively impacts sleep is by reducing stress. Regular exercise can be used to cope with stress, so instead of tossing and turning at night, people can release any pent-up stress and frustration during their workout. When it's time for bed, they are physically tired, they've had an emotional release, and they are ready to sleep.

That being said, strenuous workouts just before bed are generally not recommended. Even with a post-workout cooldown, the body needs time to recover. Rushing to bed right after a workout may result in trouble falling asleep as the body tries to cool off and reset to its pre-workout state. It is recommended to end an evening workout at least one hour before bedtime to limit sleep disruptions.

There are other mental health benefits associated with aerobics too. During aerobic exercise, the body releases hormones called endorphins, which not only relieve pain but also lead to feelings of relaxation and happiness. Exercise also reduces hormones such as adrenaline and cortisol, which are both linked to stress. Mental health benefits of aerobics include reduced anxiety and depression, increased positive mood and outlook, improved self-esteem, increased self-awareness, and the development of positive coping skills.

VIRTUAL WORKOUTS

Modern virtual workout options include apps, subscription services, websites, and virtual reality (VR) games. Subscription services usually have a variety of workout options, such as the chance to work out live with other subscribers and trained instructors. But these services also cost money and sometimes require special equipment, such as specific brands of stationary bikes or treadmills. The virtual fitness market is expected to continue growing and is projected to be worth more than $106 billion by 2030.[4]

Fitness apps can be paid or free, and some phones come with fitness apps already installed. YouTube, TikTok, and Instagram are all popular platforms for fitness influencers to make their workout videos and are accessible to anyone with internet access. However, anyone can start a YouTube channel or create social media accounts and upload videos, so it's important when working out virtually to make sure that the instructor is certified and teaches proper form.

Another option is VR workouts. These are done using a VR headset with controllers. VR workouts can create an

Many people choose to work out at home by taking virtual classes on their computers or televisions.

exciting, immersive experience. VZfit, one of the most popular VR workouts, includes immersive bike rides that use Google Maps to provide real surroundings to users. However, the headsets are often expensive, and VR workout apps and games must be purchased in addition to the gear. Also, some people have reported motion sickness while using VR headsets.

HIGH IMPACT VS. LOW IMPACT

Aerobics is usually divided into two types: high impact and low impact. High-impact exercises involve greater force on the feet and joints, such as the knees and ankles. They include exercises such as running and jumping and carry a greater risk of injury to the joints than low-impact exercises. Even with a proper warm-up, injury can occur during high-impact exercise if someone does not have the proper form and puts too much pressure on one or more joints.

"Low-impact exercises minimize the forces that often 'rattle the joints' and put excess 'wear and tear' on the

Many people use high-impact exercises as an effective way to train for an upcoming competition.

body," says trainer Lynsey Price.[5] These exercises are often recommended for those who are recovering from an injury or illness. They are also useful to those who are new to working out. Low-impact exercises include walking, swimming, and biking.

Some people prefer a combination of high-impact and low-impact aerobics. A person may have one or two high-impact workouts during their week and then allow their joints recovery time with low-impact exercises on other days. Whether doing high-impact or low-impact exercises, the importance of warm-ups and cooldowns remains the same.

FUELING UP

The body needs energy to have a successful aerobics workout. That fuel can come from nutrients such as protein and carbohydrates. Carbohydrates can be found in whole grains such as pasta and rice. They are also present in fruits such as bananas and apples. Protein can be found in foods such as chicken, fish, nuts, and eggs.

A meal containing carbohydrates and protein should be eaten approximately three to four hours before a workout to give the body enough time to digest the food and utilize the energy for the workout. A carbohydrate snack can be eaten approximately an hour before the workout to provide an additional burst of energy.

Foods to avoid within an hour of exercising are those high in fat and fiber. These digest more slowly, so they won't provide the energy you need in time for the workout. Fiber can cause bloating and gas, making a workout uncomfortable. Eating during a workout is usually not necessary. However, if someone is participating in a long workout, competition, or marathon, they can eat an additional carbohydrate snack to maintain energy.

After a workout, the body needs to recover. This involves eating additional carbohydrates, protein, and fats. The carbohydrates help replenish what has been burned up in the workout, and the protein aids in

muscle recovery. Fats also help the body refuel, and many
are found in high-protein foods, such as nuts, seeds,
soybeans, eggs, and fish. A well-balanced meal should
be eaten two to three hours after the workout along with
additional snacks as needed.

STAYING HYDRATED

Proper hydration also helps prepare the body for a
successful aerobics workout. The body is largely made
up of water, and drinking plenty of water is critical for
healthy function. Water helps regulate body temperature.
It also provides moisture to the nose, eyes, and mouth.
Lastly, water delivers nutrients and oxygen to cells, helps
with joint mobility, and helps flush waste from the liver
and kidneys.

Many people make the mistake of waiting until after a
workout to start hydrating. It takes time for water to move
from the stomach through the body. Hydration should
begin three to four hours before a workout. Frequent
small sips are better than large swallows spaced apart.
Taking in large quantities of fluid quickly can result in
nausea or bloating due to swallowing air.

Water is best for hydration. Sports drinks may also be
used, provided they do not have a high sugar content. An
hour before the workout, a person should aim to drink
approximately eight to 20 ounces (237–591 mL) of water.[6]

A person's body loses water through sweat during a workout, so it is important to replenish. Small sips of water can be taken during short workouts. For workouts lasting an hour or more, people should aim to drink four to six ounces (118–177 mL) of water every 15 minutes.[7]

They should also continue hydrating after the workout is over. In the hour following exercise, a person should continue drinking water or a sports drink to replace fluid lost through sweat and help the body recover from the workout.

WARMING UP AND COOLING DOWN

The beginning of every aerobic workout should be a warm-up. The body needs to prepare for the workout ahead. Warm-ups should include movements to get the heart gradually pumping faster and should usually last five to ten minutes just before the workout. By the end of the warm-up, your body should feel more engaged, and your heart should be beating faster than when you started.

Cooldowns play an equally important role. After an aerobic workout, the heart rate needs to come back down to its normal resting level. The body also needs to begin the process of recovery and rebuilding. "The cooling down process after exercise leads to the re-establishment of the body's ability to function and recover, and over a long period, this leads to an improvement in performance," says physiotherapist Uzo Ehiogu.[8]

KEEPING CONSISTENT

It is important to exercise often. How often someone should participate in aerobics varies by age and

Stretching is a key element of any post-workout cooldown.

other factors. For people ages six to 17, experts recommend moderate-to-vigorous exercise for 60 minutes each day.[9] They should also include exercises that focus on muscle and bone strengthening at least three days per week, which makes aerobics a great fit.[10] Many sports, such as swimming, cycling, walking, running, and rowing, also require aerobics, so if an athlete has a practice or training session, it may count toward their aerobic activity total for that week.

People ages 18 to 64 should aim to get at least 150 minutes of fairly vigorous physical activity each week.[11] This can be broken down into 30 minutes of activity, five days per week, or someone could also opt for longer workouts on fewer days. For this age group, muscle strengthening exercises should be performed at least two days a week. Again, aerobics is a great option as it provides a cardiovascular workout while also strengthening muscles and bones.

COMMON INJURIES

Even with the proper gear and a good warm-up, sustaining an injury while doing aerobics is still possible. Some injuries, such as sprains and strains, are common across many activities. Sprains and strains can occur anywhere, from the feet and ankles to the leg muscles or lower back muscles. A sprain is a tearing of a ligament, which attaches bones together. Other injuries are specific to certain exercises. Some injuries grow worse over time due to prolonged use of the joints and muscles or from ignoring an injury and continuing to work out when rest is needed.

Common walking and running injuries include sprains, lower back strain, and plantar fasciitis. A strain occurs when a muscle or tendon is overextended and tears. Proper warm-ups and stretches before walking or running help prevent these kinds of injuries. Rest, appropriate workout length, and proper form are also preventive. If the walk or run is too long or if someone is especially tired, their technique and form might suffer as they continue. This can cause someone to slouch, lean forward, or take longer, uncomfortable steps in an effort to speed up the end of the workout.

Maintaining proper form can be difficult late in a workout, but it is an important part of preventing injury.

Plantar fasciitis is an injury to a ligament on the bottom of the foot and can result from many things, including wearing the wrong kind of shoes. Supportive walking or running shoes can help prevent this type of injury. Another good way to prevent plantar fasciitis is to stretch the calf and foot muscles well.

Common running injuries include runner's knee and shin splints. Runner's knee is a term for pain felt under or around the kneecap. Shin splints refer to pain felt in the shin while running. Both injuries can happen for many reasons, including weak muscles, improper shoes, or poor form. Another preventive step an athlete can take is strengthening muscles, particularly the adductors.

Even though biking is a low-impact exercise, it can still cause injury. Common biking injuries include knee pain, neck and back pain, foot tingling or numbness, and head injuries. Knee pain can result from overuse of the knees, or by not having the bike positioned correctly. Adjusting the distance from the saddle to the pedals may treat or prevent this injury.

Improper form while riding can result in neck and back pain. This may be avoided by adjusting the handlebars and using proper riding technique. Padded cycling shorts can also help prevent pain associated with sitting on the bike's saddle for an extended period of time. Foot pain, tingling, or numbness may be avoided by wearing properly fitted shoes or cleats. A helmet will help protect against head injuries in crashes.

Swimming is generally gentle on the body, but injuries can still occur from a swim workout. Common swimming injuries include shoulder problems, called swimmer's shoulder, and lower body problems. Swimmer's shoulder can result from an injury to the rotator cuff and tendinitis. Lower body injuries include hip pain, lower back pain, and pain to the knee due to injured tendons or ligaments. The best ways to avoid swimming injuries are using correct stroke technique, warming up properly, doing cooldowns, and taking rest days to let the body recover.

Attempting to power through the pain and keep working out can result in a worse injury and a longer healing time. Someone might be unsure as to whether they are injured or just sore. If that is the case, it is important to be safe and have an injury checked out by a medical professional before continuing exercise.

TAKE A BREAK

Aerobics is about getting active, but it's important to remember to take breaks too. Injuries or illness both require time for the body to recover. Even without an injury, rest days are still important to allow the body time to both recover and recharge. Soreness comes from overworking the muscles, and while it's important to push oneself to achieve goals and to conquer challenges, extreme soreness is the body's way of saying the workout was too demanding and recovery time is needed.

Overtraining strains the body and muscles and increases the chances of injuries. "Think of a phone, it needs to be recharged to work again at its full potential. If it doesn't have time charging, it won't work at all!" says fitness coach Fiona Simpson.[12]

A rest day might mean a day completely free from working out. However, an active rest day is also an option. If someone is used to rigorous, high-impact aerobic exercises such as running, they may want to switch to a shorter, low-impact workout on a rest day. Walking and swimming are great options for less demanding exercises that keep the body moving. A rest day could also be dedicated to stretching. The body will still benefit from the movement, and the muscles will have a chance to relax and recharge. Some choose to practice yoga on active rest days. The best rule is to listen to your body.

Yoga is a popular way to both stretch and cool down after a strenuous workout.

WALKING

Walking isn't always the first activity associated with aerobic exercise. But walking is a form of aerobics. While it may not be as high energy as some other forms of exercise such as dancing, walking still offers a great workout.

BENEFITS OF WALKING

Walking offers the same health benefits as other forms of aerobics. It provides a cardiovascular workout and builds muscle strength. Better sleep and mental health benefits can also be gained by walking as regular aerobic exercise.

Walking stands out from some other forms of aerobics because it is a low-impact exercise, which is a key reason many people choose to walk.

Walking is the most popular type of exercise in the United States.

It is also a great option for someone who is recovering from an injury or illness. If you are new to aerobics, walking is a good place to start, as it is a gentle way to help your body adjust to working out before engaging in more demanding, high-impact exercises such as running or dancing. "Walking helps make your heart more efficient," says doctor Tamanna Singh. "As you're improving your fitness, your heart actually becomes more effective."[1]

Your hamstrings, quads, calves, adductors, and glutes are all used while walking. But walking engages and strengthens more than just the legs. This exercise also activates your core muscles, such as your abdominals and the muscles that surround your spine. Your arms can also be engaged while walking. Doing so actually reduces the amount of energy it takes to walk, and swinging your arms will pump those muscles as well.

WHERE TO WALK

Walking aerobics can be done almost anywhere. It is an activity that you can easily adapt to increase difficulty. There are outdoor options such as designated tracks, walking trails, or neighborhood sidewalks. Areas with hills can be used to increase difficulty. Inside options include indoor tracks and treadmills.

Safety is always important, especially when opting to walk outside. You should always be aware of your surroundings and carry a cell phone in case you need to call for help. Wear reflectors or reflective clothing in the evening, late at night, or very early in the morning to help passing drivers spot you. If walking during the day, sunglasses, a hat, and sunscreen can be worn to protect from the sun's harmful ultraviolet (UV) rays. If you decide to wear earbuds while walking outside, it's a good idea to keep one ear free to pay attention to your surroundings.

Walking can be done alone, with a friend, or in a group. Some people enjoy walking alone because it gives them a chance to think and clear their head. Others enjoy catching up with a friend while walking, and still others like the social interaction of walking with a group. Walking with others provides extra safety while also building a community atmosphere where people can encourage one another.

WARMING UP

Although walking is less strenuous on your body than some other exercises, it is still important to warm up beforehand. A proper warm-up should prepare more than just your legs. Calf raises and quad stretches are great, but torso twists and arm stretches should be included to loosen up your whole body and prepare it for a workout.

During your warm-up, your heart rate should gradually rise, and your body should start to feel warm as it increases both blood flow and oxygen intake.

Just like with other aerobic workouts, proper eating and drinking should be practiced before a walking workout. You should start hydrating three to four hours before walking and may carry a water bottle to continue to hydrate during the walk if you like. A meal of carbohydrates and protein should be eaten three to four hours before walking, with a carbohydrate snack closer to the walk for additional energy.

A lack of proper food or hydration before walking can lead to dizziness and lightheadedness. Your body needs proper food and hydration to have the energy to sustain a walking workout, just as with other forms of aerobic exercise. Low impact does not mean low preparation.

CHOOSING A WATER BOTTLE

People have many choices when it comes to water bottles. If someone has a water bottle holder on their treadmill, outdoor bike, or stationary bike, they should measure the size of the holder to make sure the water bottle will fit. It is helpful if the water bottle is marked in measurements to help someone track how much water they drink. A carry handle on the lid is also helpful. Other possibilities include bottles that light up as a reminder to drink, water bottles with filters, and insulated water bottles to keep the water cool.

FITNESS SNAPSHOT
WALKING

Keep head up and facing forward
Keep chin parallel to the ground
Straight posture
Engage core muscles
Keep elbows bent and allow arms to swing freely
Roll foot from heel to toe upon landing

PROPER FORM

When walking for exercise, or at any other time, you should stand up straight and avoid hunching or rounding the shoulders and back. This kind of poor posture can cause back pain and make it difficult to breathe. Instead of looking down at your feet while walking, keep your head up with your chin parallel to the ground. Your core should be engaged, but your pelvis should stay neutral, meaning your back should not be arched.

Swing your arms back and forth, making sure they don't go far past your hips. Do not twist your torso as you swing your arms. It is also important to swing from the shoulders, not the elbows.

When taking steps, use your whole foot, rolling forward from heel to toe. "When you roll off the front of your foot, you want the center of pressure to come off between your big toe and your second toe," says biomechanics professor Wendi Weimar.[2] It is also important to take a smooth stride. Stretching your leg too far out in front of you as you step increases the pressure on your joints as you land.

TRACKING PROGRESS

There are many ways for people to track their walking workouts. Many smartphones have fitness apps that allow people to manually input their workouts.

Smartwatches often record step counts during workouts such as walking, and many wearable fitness devices do the same. The technology that allows them to do this is called an accelerometer. When you walk, it reads the changes in the device's position to know when you are moving. A bend of your leg with the phone in your pocket will tell the accelerometer you are taking a step, allowing it to count that motion and track your walking progress.

Smartphones and watches can also help you set new targets for your walks. There is often an option to set a daily, weekly, or monthly walking goal on these apps and devices. After reaching the goal several times, it can then be increased to progress toward a new goal.

There are also different ways to measure individual workouts. Some people like to measure a walk by the number of steps they take while others like to measure by the distance they've walked. Still others like to measure by the amount of time they've spent walking. If walking indoors, most treadmills

Studies show that taking 8,000 to 10,000 steps per day is an ideal amount, depending on a person's age and fitness level, among other factors.

offer options to track by time or distance. There is no right or wrong way to measure a workout, as individual people have different abilities and goals. What's important is to keep working toward that goal, whatever form it takes.

RUNNING

Running is the preferred exercise for millions of people, and there are many events around the world dedicated to running. Six major marathons held each year draw runners from all over the world. They are held in New York City; Boston, Massachusetts; Chicago, Illinois; Berlin, Germany; London, England; and Tokyo, Japan.[1] A marathon is a running event that is 26.2 miles (42.2 km) long. There are also several Olympic events for running, including sprints, relays, middle-distance runs, and road running.

BENEFITS OF RUNNING

Like other forms of aerobic exercise, running offers physical and mental health benefits.

Studies show that roughly 50 million Americans run as a form of exercise.

Running strengthens the heart and other muscles of the body, and it improves sleep quality as well.

Running, or a slower form called jogging, is taxing on the joints, so those with knee, ankle, or foot injuries should consider a low-impact alternative such as walking or swimming. Running is a workout for the whole body, not just the legs. While it's true that hamstrings, quads, and calves get a great workout from running, the glutes and core are also used during running, and arms are engaged as well.

Running can be done continuously or broken into intervals. If you are just starting your running journey, you may want to try intervals of running and walking. Then, as your body grows stronger, you may choose to run the entire workout and use walking as a warm-up and cooldown.

Interval running can include periods of sprinting alternating with jogging or walking.

WHERE TO RUN

Running requires no equipment and can be done just about anywhere. There are outdoor options such as roads and trails. Dedicated running tracks can be found both indoors and outdoors. There are also indoor-only options such as treadmills and elliptical machines. Ellipticals are essentially low-impact treadmills. Instead of running on a flat surface, you place your feet on special pedals. In this way, the elliptical provides a running workout that is easier on the joints.

Appropriate clothing for a runner depends on many factors, including the weather and location.

Running outdoors involves many of the same safety considerations as walking. Runners should remain aware of their surroundings, carry a cell phone for emergencies, and protect themselves from UV rays. Many runners choose to head out in the morning or evening, as these times of day are less likely to be too warm to run comfortably. Beyond the safety aspect, this also allows runners to get in a workout before or after school or work.

Many people opt to run alone, as it is a chance to have some personal time and to relieve stress. Others may choose to run with a partner or as part of a group.

Group running can be problematic if not everyone in the group runs at the same pace, but it can also provide a team spirit that is helpful for cheering each other on.

WARMING UP

As with any pre-exercise routine, runners need to eat protein and carbohydrates and drink enough water before a run to fuel and hydrate their bodies. Many runners also prefer to hydrate during their runs. Small water bottles can be carried either by hand or on a belt. Runners who are traveling longer distances sometimes carry larger bottles inside backpacks. Many of these contain straws that allow runners to drink straight from the pack without removing the bottle.

A pre-run warm-up should encompass the entire body, including legs, arms, and core. There are several stretches that can be done prior to running. Leg swings, done by putting one hand against a wall, standing on one leg, and swinging the other, are a great warm-up. Other stretches such as hip rotations and shoulder rolls

FASTEST MAN IN HISTORY

Jamaican Usain Bolt's top recorded running speed was 27.79 miles per hour (44.72 km/h).[4] He reached that mark during the 100 meters at the 2009 World Championships in Berlin, Germany. He finished the event in a world-record 9.58 seconds.[5] Bolt won eight Olympic gold medals during his career.

Stretching the quadriceps muscle, which is located on the front of the thigh, is important before and after running.

will loosen up other parts of your body. Movements such as forward skipping will both loosen your body and slowly raise your heart rate, preparing your body for the rigors of running.

PROPER FORM

"If you're . . . running with bad form, it's not going to feel good," says personal trainer Erin Beck. "But when you find proper running form, your body will feel better, and running won't be such a pain."[6] As with walking, correct running form means good upright posture with the head looking forward, not down, and the neck neutral. Your shoulders should be even, not hunched up near the ears. Engaging your core can help maintain good running posture and balance. Your arms should be engaged too, bent at a 90-degree angle and moving in a controlled, back-and-forth swing as you run.

Landing on your toes or heels can cause pain or injury, so your feet should hit the ground at about the mid-foot or on the ball of the foot. Whichever position is more comfortable and easier to push off from can be used as the landing position. Your feet should land directly under your body rather than in front of your body.

It is also important to watch how your feet land. When running, make sure your feet land in a neutral position. Pronation happens when you land and your arch rolls inward at the ankle. Supination happens when the arch rolls outward. Over time, both issues can lead to soreness and injury. Knowing how your feet land can also help you select the proper type of running shoe. Specific shoes can assist in defending against both pronation and

RUNNING

Keep eyes
forward
Head up, keep
ears in line
with shoulders
Bend elbows
90 degrees
Keep hips square
and pointing
forward
Land with feet
hip-width apart

supination by providing support to certain areas of the arch and ankle.

COOLING DOWN

An essential part of every run comes after the workout is over. After a run, your body temperature has risen, your heart rate is up, and your breathing is heavy. A cooldown is needed to return your body to its pre-running state. A great way to begin a cooldown after a run is to switch to walking. Walking for a few minutes will slow your heart rate and breathing and bring your body temperature down.

Stretching after a run can help counteract soreness. Every muscle that was utilized during the run should be stretched. To stretch your calf, stand with one leg in front of the other, then lean forward while keeping your heels flat on the ground. You should feel the stretch in the calf area of your back leg.

SHALANE FLANAGAN

Shalane Flanagan is a runner, coach, author, wife, and mother. She is a four-time Olympian who won a silver medal in the 10,000-meter race at the 2008 Games.[7] She also won the 2017 New York City Marathon. In 2014, she set a record for the fastest time ever recorded by an American woman at the Boston Marathon. She has authored three cookbooks for athletes and helps coach the cross-country team at the University of Oregon. Flanagan has more than 400,000 followers on Instagram.[8]

To stretch your hamstring, lie on your back with one leg on the ground and the other straight in the air. Keeping your leg as straight as possible, grab your lifted leg with both hands behind your knee and gently pull it toward you. The rest of your body, especially the shoulders, should remain flat on the ground. Remember to repeat each stretch for both legs.

TRACKING PROGRESS

How you track your running progress might depend on where you are running. While running on city streets, you may need only an app or smartwatch that can plan a route while tracking mileage, time, and calories burned. More advanced apps and trackers can help create running routes, but they can also create workout plans or track more complicated workout metrics. One example is VO2 max. It measures how much oxygen your body can use in a certain period of time. It is one way to measure a person's fitness and endurance. Regular workouts and training can help increase a person's VO2 max number.

Runners who are cross-training for other sports can find fitness apps and watches that can create sport-specific running workouts. There are also several devices geared specifically toward outdoor trail runners. These trackers can keep tabs on everything from air pressure to altitude. Trail runners often need to find the

quickest ways through difficult terrain. Some watches
can help point out the best way through mountainous or
densely forested areas.

BIKING

Once used solely as a form of transportation, biking has become a form of exercise beloved by many. Biking is an aerobic exercise that can be done alone or with friends. It is also a competitive sport called cycling. Biking for fitness and sport has become so popular that today there are magazines, websites, clothing, and races dedicated to biking.

BENEFITS OF BIKING

Though biking primarily engages the legs for pedaling, several other parts of the body get a workout as well. The hips, glutes, and core are also engaged while biking, which helps build their muscles. "One of the key benefits of cycling is its low-impact activity," says Peloton instructor

Roughly 55 million people ride a bike each year in the United States.

Sam Yo. "Cycling places minimal stress and pressure on your joints, making it a great option for those with injuries, joint pain, or struggles doing high-impact cardio."[1]

Like other aerobic exercises, biking provides an excellent cardiovascular workout along with other health benefits such as improvements to sleep and greater muscle strength. Mental health benefits of biking include stress management, coping skills, and a boost in positive mood.

Biking is an exercise that can be tailored to increase or decrease in difficulty on any given day. A person could pedal rigorously for an entire ride or break up a ride into fast and slow intervals. In recent years, e-bikes have provided another option for outdoor riders. The motors on these bikes can assist with uneven terrain or challenging hills. They have allowed people to ride who might normally avoid biking.

If biking indoors, many stationary bikes have

Riding while standing up helps bicyclists save energy and move uphill.

the option to set an incline to mimic riding up a hill. This allows someone to adjust the difficulty of their workout as needed. If they're looking for a challenge, a biker could turn up the resistance on a stationary bike for a more demanding workout. They can also get out of the seat and ride standing up. This is known as rising out of the saddle.

WHERE TO BIKE

Biking can be done both indoors and outdoors. Outdoor cycling is usually done on a road or bike path. These paths vary from flat surfaces to steep hills. Someone could also opt for mountain biking, which brings not only the challenge of incline and hills but also rough, uneven terrain. When riding outside, they should always take safety precautions. These include wearing proper safety gear, such as a helmet, and being aware of surroundings, other bikers, and traffic. The bike and the biker's gear should have reflectors on them to help drivers see them when it is dark. Bikers should familiarize themselves with local traffic laws and stay within designated bike lanes whenever available.

Biking can be done alone or with a friend. However, it might be tricky trying to chat with one another if biking outdoors, as there can be distractions such as traffic, other bikers, or people walking around. If biking indoors, two riders could sit on stationary bikes next to each other at a gym.

WARMING UP

As with any form of aerobic exercise, you should consume proper food and water to provide energy for the workout before riding. Three to four hours before a ride, you should have a meal of carbohydrates and protein and should begin hydrating. A snack can be eaten 30 to 60 minutes before the ride. Because biking can be rigorous, it's a good idea to bring a water bottle and continue to hydrate throughout the ride. This is especially true if you are riding outdoors on a hot day. Most stationary bikes come equipped with water bottle

holders, and many road and mountain bikes have a space where a bottle holder can be attached.

You should spend a few minutes warming up your body before your ride. The warm-up should include leg movements that activate the quads, hamstrings, and calves. The glutes and core should be warmed up too. In addition to walking, jumping jacks, or torso twists, many cycling stretches are specifically geared to mimic the motions done while riding. One such stretch is a combination of a high knee pull and a forward lunge. While standing up straight, pull one knee up to your chest while also rising up onto the ball of your other foot. From there, bring the lifted leg down and forward. Keeping the knee bent, extend into a forward lunge position until your foot hits the ground. This type of stretch, along with several others specifically for riders, will both move your body and elevate your heart rate.

PROPER FORM

It is important to make the right adjustments to the bike. The saddle should be raised or lowered so it's at the height of your hip bone when you are standing next to the bike. The saddle can also be adjusted horizontally, closer or farther from the handlebars. Position the saddle so there is a slight bend in the elbows when holding the handlebars.

While riding, keep your shoulders back and your chin down. When one of the pedals is at its lowest point, that leg should have a slight bend at the knee. It is important to move your legs in a square motion. The top of the square coincides with your leg moving from back to front. The downward pedal is at the front of the square. You then follow through front to back to form the bottom edge of the square before raising your leg back up to form the back vertical line. Using this square motion, cycling coach Alison Freeman says, "not only are your quads less fatigued because they are better supported by your calves, hamstrings, and glutes, you are also now creating more rotational force with greater efficiency."[3]

COOLING DOWN

The easiest way to start a cooldown after a ride is to slow the pace. If a rider has been using resistance on a stationary bike, they should lower the resistance. If they've been on an incline outdoors, they should find a flat area.

BIKING

Keep eyes
forward
Relax shoulders
Relax elbows
Keep spine
neutral and
back straight
Keep knees
and feet
aligned

They should slowly begin reducing their speed, which will signal to the heart that it's time to slow its pace.

After slowing for a few minutes, the biker can get off the bike and begin post-ride stretches. They should pay close attention to the legs, hips, and glutes. Targeting these muscles will help prevent soreness.

TRACKING PROGRESS

Most stationary bikes allow the rider to view their workout in distance biked as well as time spent riding. Many even show the estimated number of calories burned during the workout. In recent years, companies such as Peloton have taken the concept of the stationary bike even further. Peloton bikes are connected to online networks. Riders can track their progress against others who are riding in the same classes at the same time.

Additionally, some smartphones and smartwatches allow riders to input ride information manually. Others will automatically track rides. Devices with GPS can even track the route for outdoor rides. Tracking time and distance for a biking workout isn't mandatory. However, if someone is working to increase their fitness levels or working toward a goal such as a cycling event, a workout tracker can help them stay on course.

SEVEN

SWIMMING

Swimming can mean many different things to different people. For some, it might simply mean splashing around in the waves at the ocean or relaxing in a lake or neighborhood pool. However, to many, swimming is an excellent aerobic workout. Swimming can be done alone or with a group and can be done for fitness or as a competitive sport.

BENEFITS OF SWIMMING

Swimming is a low-impact exercise that is gentle on the body. "The buoyancy of the water takes the weight off," says exercise physiologist Christopher Travers. "It also adds resistance."[1] Exercising in water is a welcome relief for those recovering from injuries. It is also helpful for people with

Swimming is considered one of the best exercises because it works the entire body.

FITNESS SNAPSHOT
FREESTYLE
Push water with hand and forearm
Turn head to breathe
Keep body aligned, facing forward
Bend at elbow when raising arm out of water
Kick from hips

joint conditions such as osteoarthritis that make working out uncomfortable. In fact, exercising in water has been shown to improve joint pain and stiffness associated with conditions such as osteoarthritis and rheumatoid arthritis. Additionally, regular swimming has been shown to improve symptoms in women who are suffering from fibromyalgia.

Swimming is a workout for the whole body, from the shoulders, arms, and wrists down to the glutes, legs, ankles, and feet. Physical health benefits of swimming include improved cardiovascular health, endurance, and strength. Swimming is also a great option for those just starting their fitness journey who would like to progress to other exercises such as running or biking. Swimming is a gentle way for the body to get used to working out and building strength.

People who participate in swimming workouts often swim laps. However, there are many other ways to swim for exercise. Many people participate in water aerobics classes. Others work out by water walking—walking laps in a pool against the natural resistance of the water. People can work out longer in water than they can on land without increased pain in the muscles or joints. Some people enjoy swimming for this reason. They can opt for longer water workouts fewer days a week rather than a larger number of shorter workouts on land. This allows

for flexibility in scheduling and rest days to enjoy other activities.

WHERE TO SWIM

Many gyms and health centers have indoor pools for swimming and water aerobics, though a membership is typically required to use them. A person may also swim in their own pool, a community pool, or a natural body of water such as a lake, a river, or the ocean. It's important that a swimmer be aware of their surroundings, both indoors and outdoors. If inside or in a public space, they should be aware of others nearby. If outside, they should always check for inclement weather approaching, such as lightning, which makes swimming dangerous. They should wear sunscreen to protect themselves from sunburn. Wherever a person is swimming, it is important to know whether a lifeguard is on duty.

A person can choose to swim alone or with a friend or group. However, it is not possible to chat with a friend while swimming laps, as the head is underwater much of the time. But friends can swim laps alongside each other and check in with one another when breaks occur. Another option is to join a group, such as a water aerobics class, as these classes offer a swim workout with social interaction, and people get the chance to encourage one another and make friends.

COMPETITIVE SWIMWEAR

Competitive swimming created a need for form-fitting swimwear that was water-resistant and wouldn't slow swimmers down. After years of experimenting with different materials, Speedo debuted a new model of swimwear, the S2000, at the 1992 Olympic Games. Other companies have produced different swimwear, including body suits, but Speedo remains the dominant competitive swimwear brand. More Olympic medals have been won by swimmers in Speedo swimwear than in any other brand.

It is important to stretch the entire
body before a swimming workout.

WARMING UP

As with other aerobic exercises, it is important to eat a meal of carbohydrates and protein roughly three to four hours before swimming. The importance of drinking water before a swim should not be overlooked, as you sweat while doing aerobics in water just like you do on land. However, because you are working out in water, you may not realize you are sweating.

You should start drinking water three to four hours before you begin your workout. "With a lack of hydration, swimmers can experience early onset fatigue during workouts, poorer response times, an increase in the risk of injuries, and sharp rise in the risk of cramping both inside and outside the pool. Dehydration of any degree can negatively affect a swimmer's performance in the water," says swim coach Joseph Buchanan.[2]

Even though swimming is gentle on the body, a warm-up is still needed, and the upper body, back, core, and lower body should all be involved. Walking is a good way to elevate your heart rate in preparation for a swimming workout. There are several stretches that can be done to ensure your body is ready to swim. One is called a wall press. You start by putting one palm flat against a wall with your arm extended. You then turn your torso away from your arm while keeping your palm flat and your arm straight. You should feel the

BACKSTROKE

Lift one arm out of the water as the other arm rotates under the water
Keep head and neck neutral
Rotate from shoulders
Keep body flat in the water
Flutter kick with legs

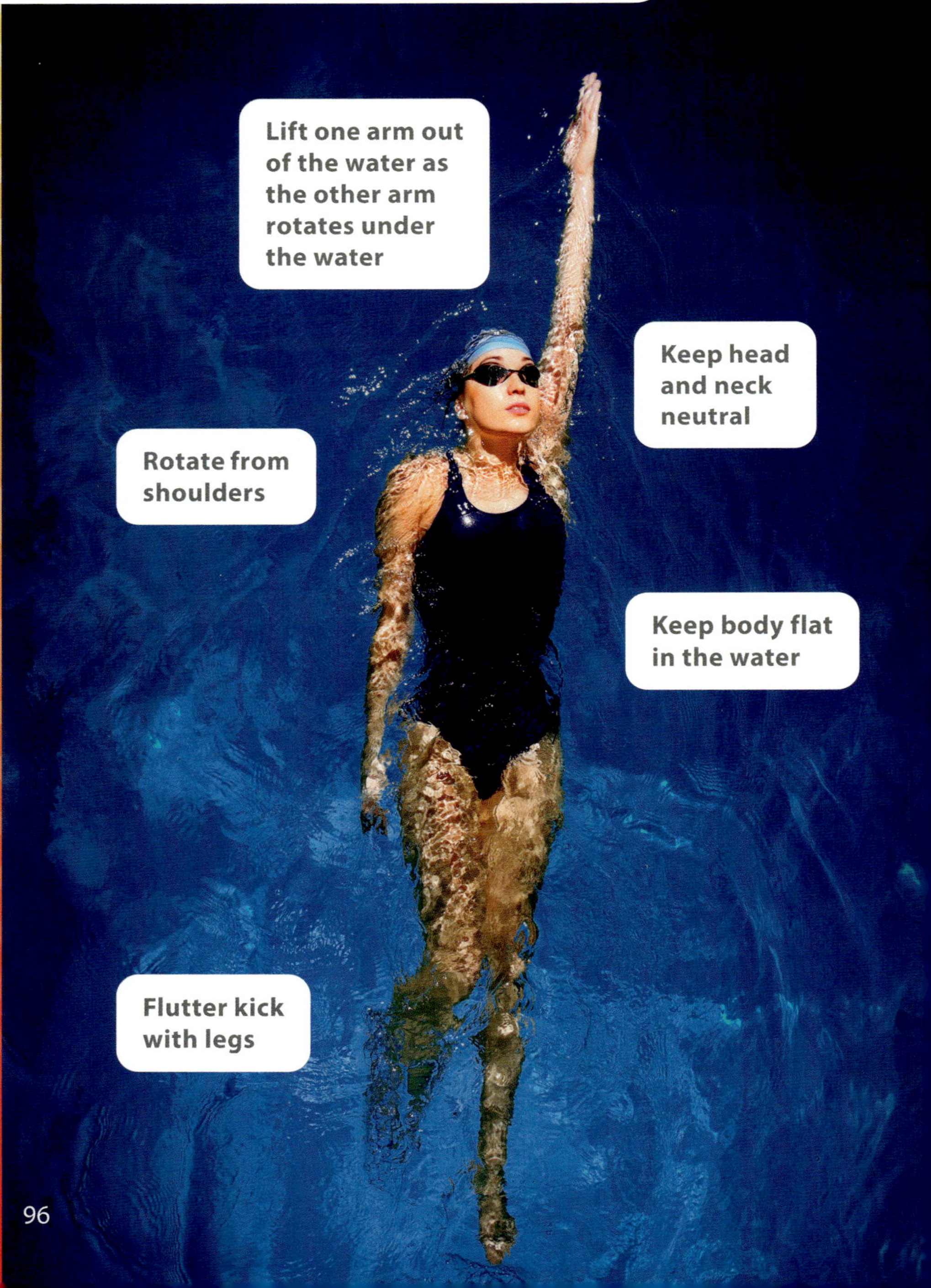

stretch in your chest
and shoulders.

PROPER FORM

Common swimming
techniques are the
butterfly, the backstroke,
the breaststroke, and
freestyle. Freestyle is the
most common stroke
used by recreational lap
swimmers. Good form
for freestyle swimming
is keeping your head and neck neutral, meaning in line
with one another. Your head should face the bottom of
the pool. One arm should reach over the water past the
head while the other arm pushes down through the water
toward the hip. Your arms should pull as alternating leg
kicks push through the water.

Keeping your feet flexible will help them act as
fins, and when your legs kick, your feet move to help
propel you through the water. When kicking in the
water, you should kick from the hips, not the knees.
Your knees should bend only slightly. Use your forearms
to move through the water instead of paddling with your
hands. Your forearms and hands should stay firm and

push against the water to pull your body forward.

COOLING DOWN

Your body stays cooler in water workouts than it does during land workouts because the water helps keep your body temperature from elevating too much. However, you still need a cooldown after a swim.

Post-swimming cooldowns are similar to cooldowns for other aerobic exercises and should involve slowly lowering your heart rate back to its pre-workout state. Stretching all major muscle groups is important to prevent soreness, and hydration should continue post-swim to help your body recover.

TRACKING PROGRESS

Common ways swimmers track their progress is by the distances they swim or the number of laps they do in a pool. Some smartwatches or wearable fitness devices are waterproof, and they can be used to track swim workouts using distance, time, and calories burned. But it's important to make sure a device is waterproof before using it in the water.

Some gyms and fitness centers have the length of their pools displayed in meters, so a person can calculate the distance they swim based on their number of laps and the number of meters per lap. Another way to track swim workouts is by the amount of time spent swimming. Someone just starting out may aim for 10 to 15 minutes of swimming. The person may then increase their workouts to 20 to 30 minutes at a time or more.

What Is Aerobic Exercise?

- Aerobics is a form of exercise that uses oxygen to power the body's heart and muscles during the workout.

- There are two types of aerobics: high impact and low impact. The difference is the amount of stress put on the joints during the workout.

- Aerobics for physical fitness was popularized in 1968 by Kenneth H. Cooper in his book *Aerobics*.

- Popular aerobic workouts include walking, running, biking, and swimming.

- Today people practice aerobics individually, with a group, or as part of a competitive sport.

Benefits of Aerobics

- Improved strength and endurance.

- Reduced blood pressure.

- Lower resting heart rate.

- Better sleep quality.

- Reduced stress.

- Relief from certain health conditions, such as osteoarthritis.

- Help prevent bone loss due to osteoporosis.

Quote

"We do not stop exercising because we grow old—we grow old because we stop exercising."

—Kenneth H. Cooper, aerobics pioneer

GLOSSARY

adrenaline
A hormone secreted by the body during times of stress.

carbohydrate
A nutrient found in foods such as pasta, rice, and fruits that is broken down by the body and used for energy.

cardiovascular
Related to the heart and blood vessels.

cortisol
A hormone released by the adrenal glands during times of stress.

endorphin
A hormone secreted by the brain that produces feelings of calm and relaxation.

fibromyalgia
A chronic health condition affecting primarily women that causes pain throughout the body.

hormone

A chemical produced by the body that creates various effects throughout the body.

osteoporosis

A disease in which the bone structure begins to deteriorate, resulting in bone loss.

rheumatoid arthritis

A disease in which the immune system attacks the body's joints, causing inflammation.

stamina

The ability to perform physical exercise for an extended time.

tendinitis

Inflammation of the tendons, which attach muscles to bones.

Selected Bibliography

"Aerobic Exercise." *Cleveland Clinic*, n.d., my.clevelandclinic.org. Accessed 22 Sept. 2023.

"Depression and Anxiety: Exercise Eases Symptoms." *Mayo Clinic*, n.d., mayoclinic.org. Accessed 22 Sept. 2023.

"Fueling and Hydrating Before, During, and After Exercise." *Nationwide Children's Hospital*, n.d., nationwidechildrens.org. Accessed 22 Sept. 2023.

"Physical Activity for Different Groups." *Centers for Disease Control and Prevention,* n.d., cdc.gov. Accessed 22 Sept. 2023.

Further Readings

Fairchild, Melody, and Elizabeth Carey. *Girls Running: All You Need to Strive, Thrive, and Run Your Best*. VeloPress, 2020.

Slomin, Jackie. *Sports Nutrition for Young Adults: A Game-Winning Guide to Maximize Performance*. Rockridge, 2020.

Turner, BJ. *Mountain Biking for Teens: Everything You Need to Know for Beginners*. Catherine/Rivers, 2022.

Online Resources

To learn more about aerobic exercise, please visit **abdobooklinks.com** or scan this QR code. These links are routinely monitored and updated to provide the most current information available.

More Information

For more information on this subject, contact or visit the following organizations:

Boys and Girls Clubs of America

1275 Peachtree St. NE
Atlanta, GA 30309
bgca.org

The Boys and Girls Club of America is a nonprofit organization dedicated to providing safe spaces for youth to experience education, learn about health and fitness, and receive mentorship to lead healthy, productive lives.

Michael Phelps Foundation

7 Ocean St.
2nd Floor
South Portland, ME 04106
michaelphelpsfoundation.org

The Michael Phelps Foundation is a nonprofit organization founded by Olympic swimmer Michael Phelps that offers services such as learning water safety, health and wellness education, and mental health assistance.

YMCA

101 W. Wacker Dr.
Chicago, IL 60606
ymca.org/contact

The YMCA is a nonprofit organization that provides health and fitness programs for young people. There are many locations throughout the United States.

Chapter 1. Work It Out

1. David Curry. "Fitness App Revenue and Usage Statistics." *Business of Apps*, 16 Aug. 2023, businessofapps.com. Accessed 9 Oct. 2023.

2. Kelyn Soong. "6 Simple Steps to Build an Exercise Habit." *Washington Post*, 2 Jan. 2023, washingtonpost.com. Accessed 9 Oct. 2023.

Chapter 2. What Is Aerobic Exercise?

1. Christina Gough. "Number of Health Clubs in the United States from 2008–2022." *Statista,* 27 Oct. 2022, statista.com. Accessed 9 Oct. 2023.

2. Boris Gojanovic. "Aerobics." *Sport & Exercise Medicine Switzerland Journal,* 11 Nov. 2019, sems-journal.ch. Accessed 9 Oct. 2023.

3. Natalia Mehlman Petrzela. "Sweating in Public: On Jane Fonda's Dance Aerobics Empire and Progressive Politics." *Lit Hub*, 3 Feb. 2023, lithub.com. Accessed 1 Dec. 2023.

4. Federica Laricchia. "Fitness Trackers – Statistics & Facts." *Statista,* 19 June 2023, statista.com. Accessed 9 Oct. 2023.

5. Zach Guzman. "How Zumba's Founders Turned a Video Made on the Beach with a Handycam into a Global Phenomenon." *CNBC,* 23 July 2018, cnbc.com. Accessed 9 Oct. 2023.

6. Guzman, "Zumba's Founders."

7. Felix Richter. "Ahead of the Game: Nike Rules the Sneaker World." *Statista,* 14 Apr. 2023, statista.com. Accessed 9 Oct. 2023.

8. Erin G. Ryan. "The Greatest Invention in Running—EVER—Is the Sports Bra." *Runner's World,* 30 Aug. 2018, runnersworld.com. Accessed 9 Oct. 2023.

9. Kelsey Maloney. "4 Benefits of Virtual Workouts and Why They're Here to Stay." *Fitbit,* 9 Dec. 2021, blog.fitbit.com. Accessed 29 Nov. 2023.

Chapter 3. Aerobics and the Body

1. "Heart Healthy for Life." *Fairfield Medical Center*, Feb. 2018, co.fairfield.oh.us. Accessed 29 Nov. 2023.

2. Deb Hipp. "Normal Resting Heart Rate by Age." *Forbes,* 21 Sept. 2023, forbes.com. Accessed 30 Nov. 2023.

3. "How Microtears Help You to Build Muscle Mass." *University Hospitals,* 5 Feb. 2018, uhhospitals.org. Accessed 9 Oct. 2023.

4. "Virtual Fitness Market to Be Worth $106.4 Billion by 2030." *Grand View Research*, Feb. 2023, grandviewresearch.com. Accessed 30 Nov. 2023.

5. Rachel Kraus. "A Fitness Trainer Explains the Difference between the Terms 'Low Intensity' and 'Low Impact'." *Well + Good,* 2 May 2023, wellandgood.com. Accessed 9 Oct. 2023.

6. "Belching, Gas and Bloating: Tips for Reducing Them." *Mayo Clinic*, 6 Jan. 2022, mayoclinic.org. Accessed 30 Nov. 2023.

7. "Belching, Gas and Bloating."

8. Stacey Carter. "Why It's Important to Cool Down after Exercise, According to the Science." *Live Science,* 22 Oct. 2022, livescience.com. Accessed 9 Oct. 2023.

9. "Physical Activity for Different Groups." *Centers for Disease Control and Prevention,* 29 July 2021, cdc.gov. Accessed 30 Nov. 2023.

10. "Physical Activity in Different Groups."

11. "Physical Activity in Different Groups."

12. Bridie Wilkins. "I Stopped Taking Rest Days and Was So Surprised. Here's Everything It Taught Me." *Women's Health,* 10 July 2023, womenshealthmag.com. Accessed 9 Oct. 2023.

Chapter 4. Walking

1. "The Health Benefits of Walking." *Cleveland Clinic,* 29 Mar. 2023, health.clevelandclinic.org. Accessed 9 Oct. 2023.

2. Stan Horaczek. "Walking Correctly Takes Work—Here's How to Improve Every Step." *Popular Science,* 27 Apr. 2023, popsci.com. Accessed 9 Oct. 2023.

Chapter 5. Running

1. Sean McAlister. "What Are the Six World Marathon Majors?" *Olympics*, 17 Mar. 2023, olympics.com. Accessed 30 Nov. 2023.

2. Erin Blakemore. "Who Invented the Marathon? It's Not as Ancient as You Think." *National Geographic*, 16 May 2023, nationalgeographic.com. Accessed 21 Dec. 2023.

3. Blakemore, "Who Invented the Marathon?"

4. "Usain Bolt." *Olympics*, n.d., olympics.com. Accessed 30 Nov. 2023.

5. "Usain Bolt."

6. Renee Cherry. "What Is the Proper Running Form, Anyway?" *Shape,* 25 July 2023, shape.com, Accessed 9 Oct. 2023.

7. "Shalane Flanagan - Profile." *University of Oregon*, n.d., goducks.com. Accessed 1 Dec. 2023.

8. Shalane Flanagan. "@shalaneflanagan." *Instagram*, n.d., instagram.com. Accessed 30 Nov. 2023.

Chapter 6. Biking

1. Tom Ward. "Keep Doing that Cycling Workout Even When the Weather Turns." *GQ*, 15 Sept. 2023, gq-magazine.co.uk. Accessed 9 Oct. 2023.

2. "About Peter Sagan." *Peter Sagan*, n.d., petersagan.com. Accessed 30 Nov. 2023.

3. Alison Freeman. "Yes, There Is a Technique to Pedaling a Bike." *Triathlete,* 19 Apr. 2023, triathlete.com. Accessed 9 Oct. 2023.

Chapter 7. Swimming

1. "Just Keep Swimming: 9 Benefits of Water Workouts." *Cleveland Clinic*, n.d., health.clevelandclinic.org. Accessed 9 Oct. 2023.

2. Joseph Buchanan. "Hydration and the Swimmer." *Swimming World Magazine*, 2 Aug. 2017, swimmingworldmagazine.com. Accessed 9 Oct. 2023.

3. "Michael Phelps." *Olympics*, n.d., olympics.com. Accessed 30 Nov. 2023.

4. Michael Phelps. "Letter from Michael." *Michael Phelps Foundation*, michaelphelpsfoundation.org. Accessed 1 Dec. 2023.

INDEX

Kaitlin Scirri

Kaitlin Scirri holds a bachelor's degree in writing from Buffalo State University and has authored more than a dozen books for children and teens.